WE ARE ALLIES!

Taimani Emerald

Feiwel and Friends

New York

Even when we don't realize it,

news is spreading everywhere.

It can be

It can be

It can be . . .

But, I have great news for you . . .

ARE YOU LISTENING?

EVERY PERSON, NO MATTER HOW SMALL, CAN DO SOMETHING TO CHANGE THE WORLD FOR US ALL

You can change the world by . . .

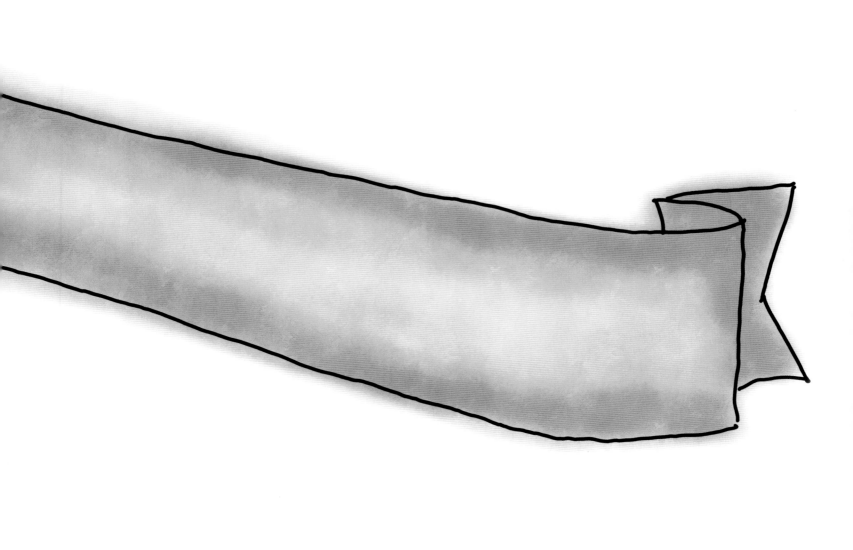

FUTURE

Being an ally means

standing up if you see someone
being treated unfairly.

Being an ally means saying sorry if something you did or didn't do hurt someone's feelings, even if you didn't mean for it to be hurtful.

how can I make the world a better place?

do I make my friends feel included?

how do I feel when I see someone treated badly?

what do justice and fairness mean in my life?

how can I be kind to someone today?

what do I see in the world that makes me sad?

how can I support my community?

what talents do I have that can help other people?

Being an ally means asking big questions and never being scared to talk about the tough stuff.

By asking, we learn.

And by learning, we can do better for ourselves and future generations!

TOGETHER . . .

Author's Note

"Mama, what's wrong?"

That is the question that inspired a movement.

I didn't start Emerald Creative and She's A World Changer because I was some fearless woman with a mission. In fact, I was quite the opposite. I was thoroughly scared, terrified to my bones watching injustice after injustice unfold before my eyes in so many different areas of my life. And while I was not, and am not, a fearless woman, I am raising a fearless little boy. Two of them, in fact.

This book was born because I, as a mother, lacked the language to verbalize what was going on in the world to my child. He said, "Mama, what's wrong?" and I had no answers. I didn't have the heart to tell him how cruel the world could be. I didn't know how to tell him that the safety and validity of every member of his family varied based off of silly things like melanin and curl pattern and the barreled shape of their nose. Or that he and his brother hold powerful privilege because they were born half white, and that someday soon, the world would need him to be a special type of person who used that privilege for good.

That the world would need him to be an ally.

So I did the only thing I really know how to do: I drew a picture. I spoke to people like you, people who want to change the world and who understand that it starts with our children, our nieces, our nephews, our students, our families, and our friends.

As a person, it is vital that we care about the humanity and celebrate the differences of all people. Then, and only then, we can create the world we wish to live in: one that is equitable, diverse, empowered, and inclusive.

Being an ally isn't just an action. It's not a list to check tasks off of. It has to be who you are. It has to be a part of your identity. You have to wake up every day and say, "I am someone who uses my privilege to stand up and take action for others."

Listen. Seek out information from historically marginalized communities, including but not limited to people of color, Muslims, immigrants, refugees, LGBTQIA+ people, women, and people with disabilities.

Learn. Thanks to social media and well-stocked libraries, there is a wealth of information at your disposal. Dedicate yourself to examining your own bias and remaining educated and involved.

Join. Give of your time by joining local groups that work toward a better world and take every opportunity to support.

If someone invites you to an event, march, or rally, go. Please. Your presence and solidarity means so much to us. It reminds us that we are not alone in our fight. That it is not us against the world.

Speak up. Use your voice to interrupt and intervene when you encounter hateful or ignorant speech and action.

You will make mistakes. It might be uncomfortable at times, but recognize that change always is. Welcome the discomfort as an opportunity to grow. You do not need to be perfect in your allyship. You just need to be committed and engaged, ready and willing to learn and move forward in creating a better world.

I started from where I was, and that is all I can ask of you. I drew a picture and magical things happened.

That picture grew into a social movement; it turned into this book, educational resources for teachers everywhere, and a center for empowerment and social enterprise. We formed She's A World Changer and sent out over a thousand anti-racist, anti-bias resources in less than six months. We were blessed with international feature. And now we continue to take an active role in empowering people of all ages to make change in their everyday lives to become better community members, stronger allies, and kinder human beings.

I drew a picture and it changed the world.

Start where you are. Use the talents you have at your disposal. Find things you like to do and give them mission, give them purpose. Take small, tangible steps every day and build up to the bigger ones as you go.

That is how you become a world changer.

TO THE BOYS WHO CHANGED MY WORLD. —T.E.

A FEIWEL AND FRIENDS BOOK
An imprint of Macmillan Publishing Group, LLC
120 Broadway, New York, NY 10271 • mackids.com

Our books may be purchased in bulk for promotional, educational, or business use.
Please contact your local bookseller or the Macmillan Corporate and Premium Sales Department
at (800) 221-7945 ext. 5442 or by email at MacmillanSpecialMarkets@macmillan.com.

Library of Congress Cataloging-in-Publication Data is available.

ISBN 978-1-250-82858-3 (hardcover)

Book design by Mike Burroughs

Feiwel and Friends logo designed by Filomena Tuosto

First Edition—2023